Curvy for Him

The Teacher and the Trainer

BY

Annabelle Winters

Copyright Notice

Curvy for Him

The Teacher and the Trainer

1

<u>ASTRID</u>

"Mrs. Astrid, your pants are torn," says nine-year-old Paulina from the front row as I hastily slip my phone back into my bag. I shouldn't be nervously staring at a dating app while in class. What kind of example does that set for the women of our future?!

"It's *Miss* Astrid, not Mrs.," I say sweetly to Paulina. "I'll be sure to invite you to my wedding when I get married."

"Mrs. Astrid's getting married! Mrs. Astrid's getting married! Mrs. Astrid's getting married!" comes the chorus from Paulina and her three front-row friends, and then suddenly my classroom bursts into uncoordinated applause punctuated by the squeaks and shrieks of nine-year-olds.

I take a long, slow breath, feeling the blood rush to my face. I love these kids, but this job has taken its toll on me, and sometimes I hate it. I don't eat right. I don't sleep enough. I don't get paid enough. Um, why am I doing this?

Mrs. Astrid's getting married! comes the chant from my classroom of girls, and I remember why I'm doing this. It's to help raise these girls right. Yes, you heard me: *Raise* these girls. Parents can only do so much. Once school starts, a child's friends and teachers have as much a role as the parents and siblings. Maybe more, depending on the parents.

I smile and shake my head, waiting for the kids to settle down. It's only then that I remember what Paulina said before the room erupted with news of my imaginary wedding.

"Wait, my pants are torn?" I say as the blood rushes to my face again. I remember wriggling my big ass into these pants this morning, but I don't remember hearing a . . . oh, wait, I do.

I bury my face in my hands, pressing my thighs together as I feel the rip down the back seam of these slacks. I should've known better than to try to get into these without pulling on some Spanx first, but I was running late and I thought maybe I could do it. I couldn't have put on *that* much weight over the past six months since I got these, right? And why does my weight go right to my ass?!

Oh wait, it doesn't, I remind myself as I glance down at my enormous thighs that I swear are hanging off the sides of this generously sized wooden chair. Of course, I can barely even see my thighs, because my freakin' boobs are in the way!

Again that feeling of despair rushes through me—a feeling that's been hitting me more and more these days. I'm sure it has nothing to do with the fact that I'm in my thirties now. Nope. There's no clock ticking. I have plenty of time to meet someone and have a child, start a family, do all those things that these girls believe are part of a woman's destiny, her meant-to-be, her happily ever after.

And they do believe that, I realize as I sigh and scan the glowing faces of my girls. They've all been raised on Disney movies where the girl gets her prince in the end. Yes, the Disney princesses are a bit less help-less nowadays, with more self-confidence. But they're still princesses.

I wanna be a princess. Just once. Just fucking *once*!

I feel a pout coming on as I slouch in my chair, wait-ing for the bell to ring so I can slink to the restroom and . . . and do what? Sew my split seam back togeth-er? Put a patch on it like some orphan in a cartoon? How about a row of safety pins? Oh God, where did I go wrong? What have I done to deserve this?!

OK, stop that self-pity nonsense, I tell myself firm-ly. You are *not* a victim! You're smart, witty, and per-sonable. These kids love you, and you're a positive role model in their lives. They need to see that a woman can be happy and fulfilled on her own. A woman doesn't need a man to complete her. A prin-cess shouldn't aspire just to be a prince's bride. She should aspire to be Queen!

"Hey, Astrid?" comes the Queen's voice, and I turn my head so sharply towards the classroom door that I swear I hear something crack in my tensed-up body. I hope that was a good crack.

"Oh, hi, LuAnn," I say hurriedly. LuAnn is our prin-cipal, but we all call her the Queen. She's good at her job and fair with her teachers; but she's also a stickler for rules and discipline. Old fashioned up the wazoo as well. "We're just . . ."

Mrs. Astrid's getting married! comes the chant again from the little monsters in the front row, and I just close my eyes and wonder if I'm going to burst out laughing or just explode into hysterical tears.

Just then the bell rings, and the girls jump out of

their seats and head for the playground. It's recess, and a moment later I am alone with the Queen, the echoes of *Mrs. Astrid's getting married!* still bouncing off the light blue walls.

"What was that about?" says LuAnn, slowly walking to the front of the desk and stopping, her hands on her tight, boyish hips, her lips pursed in a quizzical smile. "Are you really getting—"

"No!" I say, snorting as I raise my hands and shake my head. "Of course not!"

LuAnn sighs and tilts her head in a show of pity. I hate pity. I don't do pity. "You know," she says in that annoyingly pedantic voice that reminds me she stood in front of a classroom for twenty years before becoming principal, "there's nothing wrong with wanting to be married, wanting your prince, your happily ever after."

"Who said there's anything wrong with it?" I say, that pout making my face feel puffy. I try to suck in my cheeks, but it doesn't work. "All I said was—"

"It wasn't *what* you said," says LuAnn. "It was *how* you said it."

I cross my arms over my breasts and set my jaw tight. I am *not* listening to a lecture from the Queen. But shit, I can't stand up and walk out with a split butt-seam, can I? I don't want to get a lecture on proper classroom attire!

"And how did I say it," I say sullenly, settling in for a fight.

"Like it's an insult to suggest that you might actually want to get married. That's not the attitude I want to teach these girls."

"Oh, so you want to teach them that they're all princesses and should spend their lives trying to marry a prince?"

LuAnn stares at me expressionless. "They *are* all princesses. And no, I don't want them to think that finding a partner is all there is to life. But it's a big part of life." She pauses, her face softening in a way that throws me off-guard. "And for some, it's the *biggest* part of life."

I grimace as I feel LuAnn building up to the grand finale. I've heard this lecture before. LuAnn's been married since she was nineteen, and she's still married, still happy, still in love—or so she says. Four kids and thirty years later. It's a beautiful story, but not the one I want to hear right now.

But the lecture doesn't come, and I frown as LuAnn pulls out her phone and taps on it a few times. She takes a breath, nods, and then taps once more before looking up. "There," she says. "Check your messages."

I blink as I hear my phone beep in my bag. "OK, I don't do setups or blind dates," I call after the Queen as she glides to the door like she's riding a cloud. "You aren't my fairy godmother, LuAnn!"

LuAnn stops at the doorway, her tight butt on display. She turns her head and glances down along her super-fit body and then back up at me. "You want to know why my husband still wants to fuck me after thirty years?" she says softly, her language shocking me because I don't think I've ever heard the Queen drop the f-bomb.

It takes me a moment to understand what she's trying to tell me, and when I get it, I almost throw a dry-erase marker at my principal. "Did you just call me fat?!" I say in horror, blinking as I try to process what just happened. I've been curvy all my life, and it took me years to become comfortable with my body, to be just fine with the fact that I'll never be a skinny supermodel or a beach bunny, that I'll always have ripples of cellulite along my thighs, a couple of tires around my belly, boobs that will make my back hurt, a butt that seems to have a mind—and a zip code—of its own. And now this skinny bitch with a genetically engineered ass dares to—

"You know that I neither engage in nor tolerate body shaming at this school," LuAnn says firmly. "But I also care about my teachers and staff, about their happiness. A happy teacher is a good teacher. Just give it a try, Astrid. Just give it a try."

She walks out, and I shake my head in fury, my jaw set so tight I feel my teeth grinding against each other. I want to scream at LuAnn, but I force myself to take several long breaths until I calm down enough to consider what she said. What she said about happiness, not my ass.

Have I been sabotaging my own chances to find a man, I wonder as I slowly reach for my phone. Do I want what LuAnn has? A happy marriage, kids and family, a husband who can't get enough of my ass?

Maybe . . .

Perhaps . . .

Yes.

Yes, I want that.

Oh, *God*, I want that!

Allowing myself to admit it makes me choke, and then I just burst out sobbing, the tears rolling down my cheeks and plunking onto the tabletop like it's raining. I let myself cry for a minute, and then I set my jaw again and nod. To hell with feeling insulted. LuAnn wants the best for me, even if she can be blunt sometimes. I'll give it a try.

"Give *what* a try?" I wonder as I look for LuAnn's text. Some kind of new diet? OK, I am *not* drinking kale juice or eating avocado ice-cream sweetened with stevia. There are limits to what I'm willing to do.

Give us a try! is the headline when I click on the link in LuAnn's text. *Your body will thank us! So will your boyfriend! Visit Body by Armand for a free session today!*

"Your boyfriend will thank us? OK, that's obnoxious," I mutter as I scroll down and realize that LuAnn has sent me a gift certificate that gives me ten free personal training sessions at *Body by Armand*. It's also linked to her membership, which means she'll probably know if I don't take her up on the offer. What to do? Give me a sign, someone! What should I do?!

As if in response, my phone pings as my dating app scores a match. I quickly switch over, my heart racing as I wonder if that's my prince! Of course, the moment I see his picture I decide it's a frog, not a prince. Perhaps a toad, based on that double-chin. And what's with the video-game t-shirt with food-stains on it? Also, is that a beard or did a rat die on his face?!

I crack myself up, but it doesn't escape me that

I'm being judgmental as hell. Perhaps the dude is a wonderful man, kind and sensitive, intelligent and engaging. Is it right for me to dismiss him based on a bad photograph? Shit, I'm no better than some player dude who grunts and swipes left because the chick isn't hot enough or her boobs aren't big enough or whatever. I should give it a try, shouldn't I?

But I know I won't do it. No offence to Toad-face, but I have standards. And yes, looks are part of it, much as I hate to admit it.

"OK, fine, LuAnn," I say out loud as I flip back to *Body by Armand*. "I'll give Armand a try." I hesitate a moment, and then force myself to quickly sign up for my first session, clicking the "Submit" button before I have a chance to talk myself out of it.

Then I click over to the page where it lists all the personal trainers, hoping to find a chunky woman trainer who won't make me feel self-conscious. But there's only one profile on the entire page.

"You're kidding me," I say, wriggling in my chair as I stare into the fiercely confident eyes of Armand himself. "Oh, shit, what have I gotten myself into?! I can't do this!"

Nervousness flows through me like a river, and I quickly go back to the appointment page, wondering if I can cancel. Yeah, Toad-face is below my level. But Armand is clearly out of my league.

"Out of my league?" I say out loud, almost laughing when I remind myself that I'm not going on a date with Armand! It's business!

Business that involves tight clothes, heavy breathing, and sweaty, glistening bodies, I think as my breath catches at the grayed-out "Submit" button at the bottom of the screen. I flip back to that photograph of Armand, feeling a wave of heat pass through me as I stare transfixed, the word "Submit" repeating itself in my mind like a broken record, a CD with a scratch on it, a sign from the universe perhaps.

"Submit to Armand," I drone out in a fake French accent, trying to make myself laugh, to lighten up a bit. But I can't lighten up. Those eyes did something to me. It's like I already know him. It's like I already want him. It's like I already . . . love him?

OK, now you know you've been without a man too long, I tell myself as I hear the recess bell ring. You see one airbrushed photograph of a hunky dude and you're like, "OMG, he's the one!" What are you, some lovesick teenager swooning over a celebrity? Armand is probably some boneheaded loser with big biceps and shriveled up balls from all the steroids!

"What the hell is wrong with me?!" I mutter out loud as the sounds of children running back towards the classroom gets louder. "Am I turning into some bitter woman who's blaming everyone else for the fact that I'm still single, still alone, still so far from being—"

"Will you really invite me to your wedding?" comes Paulina's squeaky voice from my left, and I just burst into a big, beaming smile, pulling the innocent girl into my bosom and hugging her hard. I'm probably breaking all kinds of school rules, but what the hell.

"Of course I will," I say as I try to hold back tears. "You'll be my flower-girl! How does that sound?"

Paulina nods excitedly, and then she is back with her friends, all of them chattering about something that's either Pokémon or Paw Patrol or Facebook or Snapchat. I have no idea.

Submit to Armand, I think in my fake French accent, and this time it does make me chuckle. I picture those gorgeous eyes of his going cross-eyed as he lifts some weights the size of a truck, and I laugh again as I feel my anxiety leave me. It's not a date, I tell myself. He's just some muscle-bound dude who runs a gym. Probably never read a book in his entire life. Bet his name isn't even Armand—it's probably Pete or Quentin. Maybe Ernest. Yeah, let's go with that. Ernie! How can you be nervous about meeting a guy named Ernie?!

"Submit to Ernie," I growl to myself as the kids finally settle down in their seats. "Submit!"

2
<u>ARMAND</u>

"Never submit! Never surrender! Never yield!" I roar at the gaggle of women who are pumping their legs as hard as they can in my spinning class. I hate this class. Sitting on a stationary bike isn't my thing. But it's solid exercise, and you can get that burn going nice and strong. Besides, I'm running a business, and I need to give my customers what they want. Not everyone wants to just do weight-machines and sprint-intervals on the treadmill.

"Oh, fuck, Armand! I think I'm dying!" gasps one of my customers, a young mom in a blue tank top and pink tights. I frown at her and shake my head.

"Language," I say, keeping my breathing steady and my eyes focused on her. "Losing control of your language is the first sign of defeat. And we do not come here to be defeated, do we, ladies?"

"No!" comes the response in chorus, and I grin wide and jack up the music—some heavy metal band from Germany. They sound like animals gone wild (the band, not my customers), and I roar in delight as I feel my muscles flex and pump.

The women howl back in response. They know we're on the last leg of our class, the final segment, the big burn. I'm going to take them to the edge of their abilities, and then push them over that edge! They're going to see what they're capable of doing,

what their bodies—fat, thin, and everything in between—are capable of doing!

"*Push it!*" I roar as the music ratchets up to its cre-
scendo and the women are screaming in pain as their
thighs and calves burn through every last drop of fuel.
I know they've already burned through all the sugar they've pumped into their bodies, and now their
bodies are forced to use fat as fuel. They'll be burning
fat the rest of the day, even while watching Netflix!
"To the edge, Ladies!"

The music crashes to an end in an ear-shattering
barrage of drums, and I raise my hand to signal that
we're done. The women cheer, and then the room
descends into groans as they slide their sweaty asses
off the bikes and collapse on the floor-mats, writhing
around like they're having near-death experiences. I
hate spinning, but I love this scene. I love seeing people push themselves beyond what they believed they
could do. Yeah, I love it. Better than sex.

I blink as I glance at the women in tights and tank-
tops sweating all over my floor. There was a time
when I'd have taken my pick from these women—
married or not, customers or not. But that time has
passed. I haven't had sex in over a year, and I'm not
going to crack now.

Crack, I think as I try not to stare at one of the
women who goes up on her knees and raises her ass
in the air, letting out a huge groan that's most certainly for my benefit. I know how the human body
works, and I know that when you get that heartrate
up, get that blood pumping, you get *everything* going.

"Never yield," I mutter to myself, looking away from

the shameless display of ass on my gym floor. This chick isn't my type anyway. She's fit as hell, but too small for me. Tight butt, yeah. But nothing to hold on to. A man needs something to hold on to.

I feel my cock move in my shorts, and I turn away to grab a towel. In my mind I see her, a woman with curves sculpted in heaven, nice big ass that shudders when I spank it, boobs that burst out of her bra when I rip her top off, nipples as big as saucers, dark red and erect, glistening with my saliva as I suck them until they stand up straight like arrowheads.

I grin and shake my head. I'm used to these fantasies invading my mind. Thing is, I don't know who that woman is! It's not some ex of mine! It's not some celebrity! It's just a fantasy-woman that my sex-deprived brain has conjured up! It's just my balls reminding me that I need to unload them inside a woman who can take me, take *all* of me!

I groan as my cock hardens to almost full-mast, pushing against my shorts and forming an obscene peak at the front. I pushed myself pretty hard today, and I'm feeling fitter than ever. When you're fit, your body wants to do what comes naturally. It wants to do what comes *most* naturally:

Put its seed in a woman.

"You wanna get some, Armand?" says one of the women from behind me, and I blink and look down at myself, wondering if they've seen the tent at the front of my shorts.

"What?" I say without turning, draping the long towel over my shoulder so it covers my erection.

"Falafel," comes the reply. "We're all going to that

new Middle-Eastern restaurant at the end of the block. You wanna come get some falafel with us?"

"I have a meeting," I say hastily, turning my head sideways and smiling. "See you all on Thursday."

"If we're alive," one of them says, sighing as she slowly walks to the women's locker room. "You almost killed us today, Armand. And to think we're actually *paying* you to do this to us!"

I smile as their words hit home in a way I wish they didn't. Getting paid to kill? You have no fucking idea, lady. No fucking idea.

A darkness settles over me as I think about the meeting scheduled for this afternoon. It's a meeting that shouldn't be happening. I've been making my payments, and the deal was I'd be left alone. Left alone to think upon my sins. Left alone to heal. Left alone to put myself back together. To un-break what was broken.

I wait for my customers to leave, and then I lock the front door and head to the showers. I step out of my shorts, toss my soaked shirt against the wall, slam my palms against the cool tiles and turn on the jets. Cold water. Ice cold. Like the blood in my veins. The cold blood of a killer.

The doorbell sounds just as I find myself slipping into that dark, desolate place in my mind, the place I've been trying to shut down, to escape from. That's what all of this is for: The legitimate business thing. Doing something that I'm passionate about. Denying myself sex so I can focus on my mind, my goddamn soul!

"But these motherfuckers won't leave me alone!" I roar as I grab a towel and wrap it around my waist. The water drips down my massive pectorals in heavy beads as I walk out to the front door. These bastards are early. The goddamn cable guy will make you wait all day, but the mafia shows up early. Fuck my life.

I yank open the front door, still dripping wet, nothing but a towel around my waist. I considered dressing, but I don't want anyone else seeing a bunch of Mafioso thugs standing outside my front door. That won't be good for business.

"Um, hi!" comes a woman's voice as I pull the door open so hard it almost smacks me in the face. But one look at her and I *feel* like I've been smacked in the face! Smacked hard! Smacked by fate! By destiny! By the cupids themselves!

It's her!

The woman from my fantasy!

I swear it's her!

"Motherfucker," I gasp, my eyes going wide as I take in the sight of the woman standing in my doorway. Big brown eyes that feel familiar even though I've never looked into them before. Pretty round face that makes me weak in the knees. A bosom that's bursting through her black, shapeless T-shirt—a shirt that can't hide her shape! And hips that I just want to slam into, right here, right now! "Motherfu—"

"Um, language!" she says, blinking in shock even though her voice is steady. I can tell she's glanced down along my body, and I swear I noticed her do a double-take when she saw the way my towel was peaking at the front. Why didn't I just jerk myself off in the shower?!

"Who the hell are you?" I say, my mind swirling as I try my damndest to calm down. This whole abstaining from sex has clearly driven me insane. I'm now imagining that a woman from my dreams has shown up at my door?! You've lost it, Armand. You're beyond rescue.

"Astrid," she says, her eyes wide as if she's trying desperately to stay focused on my face and not my body. I can already sense her heat rising. Not sure how, but I feel it. I fucking *smell* it!

"Astrid," I say, my jaw clenching as the most primal need rips through my body. My cock is throbbing behind that towel, and I breathe deep as I try to control myself. A part of me wants to grab her by the hair, pull her into my gym, toss her down on the floor-mats, and jam my face between her thighs! Actually no. It's not a *part* of me that wants to do that. It's *all* of me!

And then it happens. Just as I say her name. Just as I look deep into her eyes. Just as I pick up the scent of her body, inhale that devastating mix of a floral body spray and her clean perspiration, breathe deep of what I swear is the aroma of her sex, it happens.

I come in my pants.

Or rather, I come in my towel.

I stagger as my cock explodes against the thick cotton of the towel, grabbing on to the doorframe as my eyes roll up in my head and my orgasm hits me like a sledgehammer. I don't understand what's happening, but I can't stop it. I know that holding back from sex and masturbation gets you backed up, and I've had a couple of wet dreams over the past year. But coming like this, like a horny schoolboy who sees his first booby-pic? Never happened. Not until now. Not until *her*!

"Ohmygod," she says, gasping as she takes three steps back and covers her mouth. "Oh, my *God*!"

"Fuck," I groan as my balls push out the rest of my load, my cock jerking against the towel like an animal trying to break free. "Astrid."

But she's already halfway down the block, her hand still covering her mouth, her divine ass bouncing as she walks away from me as fast as she can. I stare dumbfounded at the woman from my fantasy walking out of my life, and then I turn sharply to the left as I see my nightmare walking in.

It's Gustav's men. Four of them. All armed. All dangerous.

"All about to die," I mutter as I slip back into the gym and race to my office where I keep my gun. I'm almost out of my mind with the shock of what just happened, and I'm close to losing it. I gave it a try, didn't I? Tried to go straight. But there's no getting out. No running away from who I am. That woman was just the devil messing with me. Reminding me that I don't deserve happiness. I've taken too many lives. There's no salvation for me. No hope.

I'm cocked and loaded by the time I hear Gustav's men push open the unlocked front door and walk into my gym. My towel has fallen off, but I don't give a shit. This will all be over in a few seconds, anyway.

I can take out two, maybe three of these guys. But four is too many. Today's the day I die. Makes sense that I saw an angel first, doesn't it?

I smile as that image of Astrid comes back to me, and to my surprise I realize that I'm getting hard again even though my cock is still oozing! I stare down at myself, still smiling as I wonder if I've lost control of my body. I'm holding a loaded gun, getting ready to fight for my life, and my cock is merrily sticking out like it just wants to—

"Oh hell, he's lost it," comes a voice from in front of me, and I look up to see all four of Gustav's collectors standing aghast outside my open office door.

"Fuck, Armand! You gonna shoot us with that thing?" says Number Two.

"Yeah, put the gun away!" says Number Three.

"He means *that* gun, not the one in your hand," quips Number Four with a grin. "Holy shit, Armand. You crazy, man?! What're you on?"

I lower my gun and shake my head. It does feel like I'm on something. The greatest drug of all. A drug that makes men do crazy things. Always has. Always will.

"Sorry," I grunt, shaking my head again as I realize this isn't a hit on me. Hell, these guys had told me they were coming! And I was about to start spraying bullets all over?! What did I expect was gonna happen? Fuck, I really have a death wish, don't I?

Number One exhales as I put the gun down on the table. "You were seriously going to pop us off in a business meeting?" he says. "You've lost your edge, bro. Too long on the outside."

"What's this about?" I say, regaining my self-control, if not my dignity. Still, I don't make a move to cover myself. I know it's making these assholes uncomfortable, and that works in my favor.

"How 'bout you cover that schlong first before we get down to business," says Number One.

"Nope," I say without flinching. "This meeting ain't gonna take long."

Number One sighs and shakes his head. He looks me dead in the eye. I remember this guy. We didn't work together much—hitmen tend to work alone, in the shadows. But he had a reputation. This fucker toyed with his targets. A sadist through and through. I killed for a living, yeah. But I never took pleasure in it the way this guy did.

"Fine," says Number One, glancing at his buddies, who spread out towards the exits of my small gym. My heart almost stops as I imagine what might happen if Astrid walks back in! But then I get that sinking feeling when I realize that she isn't walking back in. Not after my display of . . . of whatever the hell that was!

And what *was* that, I wonder, my mind drifting back to Astrid's brown eyes, her red lips, those smooth round cheeks, her beautiful bosom. Hell, I'm around beautiful women every day, many of whom shamelessly come onto me. But my body's never reacted like that! That was unreal! Fucking *insane*!

My mind is clouding up as I feel arousal rush through my body once again. With a grunt I turn and grab a fresh towel from the stack on the shelf (this is a gym—I keep towels everywhere). I don't want to push my luck here. Number One might take it personally if I get hard right now.

"Gustav's calling in his favor," says Number One as I finally focus back on the real world. He tosses a brown manila envelope on the desk. Not another word. The message has been delivered.

My jaw tightens as I stare at the brown envelope. I suspected this day might come, but I had to roll the dice and do it anyway. It was the only shot I had for going straight. You don't get to make a clean break from the mob unless you disappear, and I didn't want to spend my life looking over my shoulder. So I bought my way out. That was the deal Gustav put on the table: Pay me to set you free, Soldier!

And the payment was a promise.

A promise to do one more job for Gustav.

I close my eyes as the Gustav's goons file out of my office. A moment later I'm alone in the gym. Alone again. So fucking alone.

I feel something in me reach out for her, for Astrid, a woman I don't even know! Am I so weak that I'm yearning for some chick to come take away the pain, to make me feel less lonely, less alone?!

"No!" I roar, slamming my fists down on my desk, making that brown envelope jump up like it's mocking me. This shouldn't be a big deal—hell, I've taken so many lives that one more shouldn't matter. But it does. For some reason it does. I turned my back on the man I was, and I don't want to go back there. I want to walk away from my past. I want my future.

Again a vision of Astrid floats through my mind, and I begin to pace furiously through my gym, shaking my head and muttering like a madman, rubbing my eyes and forehead as I try to calm down. I know that whatever I think I feel for this woman is an illusion. It's just a reflection of my own weakness, my own fear, my own loneliness. There's no such thing as love at first sight. No such thing as fate, destiny, or whatever the fuck else this feels like. She's just another woman, and she's gone.

Gone.

3
ASTRID

"Why aren't you gone, you dumb cow?" I mutter to myself as I stare at Armand's gym from across the street. I *was* gone—for a moment, at least. I mean, the guy is a freak! He opens the door half naked, with a boner the size of a caveman's club! And then . . . then . . . OMG, did he seriously . . .

I close my eyes and swallow hard, trying desperately to push away that feeling I'd gotten when Armand came right there, right in front of me! It should have felt disgusting, sick, perverted. But it didn't. It felt innocent. Pure. Perfect.

It felt like fate.

"Well, then fate is one sick, twisted creature," I whisper to myself. I'm smiling even though I don't want to be smiling. My body is tingling with excitement even though I want to be horrified. My feet are firmly planted on the ground even though common sense tells me I should be far, far away from this man!

I'm standing near a streetlamp, holding on to the metal pole like I'm hiding. It's moronic, since I'm way too wide to be hidden by a freakin' lamp-post! But it makes me feel better. I'm still not sure why I'm not halfway across town by now, and I shake my head as I summon up the will to turn my back and walk away. Why does it feel so hard to turn and walk away?

In the midst of arguing with myself, I hear voices, and I gasp when I see four men walking into Armand's gym. These guys aren't dressed for a workout. They're in shiny suits, all of which have suspicious bulges near their shoulders. They look like thugs. Well-paid thugs—not street hoodlums.

"What the hell?" I mutter as I hear raised voices come through to me. Now I'm scared. Am I about to witness a crime? Is Armand a criminal? Why am I still here?! Why aren't I gone?!

But I'm glued to my spot behind the lamp-post, that excitement rising up in me again. The shock of what happened with Armand has faded, leaving me burning with an arousal so fierce it scares me. It's like my body doesn't give a rat's ass about common sense and logic. My body wants to feel Armand's hands all over it. My body wants to feel Armand inside it. Deep inside. All the way inside.

I gasp as I feel my eyes glaze over, and a moment later I realize my panties are wet. I want to touch myself, and now I know I've lost my mind! Seriously, what am I doing?! I'm a teacher at a girl's school! I'm a role model for America's future women! I'm . . . I'm . . . I'm . . . his.

I'm his.

Just then the door to Armand's gym opens again, and the four men walk out of there. A moment later they've gotten into a black Range Rover and they're gone. They're gone, but I'm still here.

I can see Armand through the big glass windows of

his gym. He's still half-naked, a towel wrapped around him like a toga. I swear he looks like a Greek god of myth, with pectorals like slabs of granite, ab muscles so ribbed and defined I can count them from across the street, arms thicker than my thighs (well, probably not—but it sure as hell looks that way from here!).

Armand is muttering to himself, and from the way he's pacing I can tell he's upset. I want to go to him. I want to understand him. I want to be there for him.

"And that's why you should turn around and walk away," I tell myself in the sternest teacher-voice I can muster. "You don't know this man, and there's no way you're actually feeling what you think you're feeling! Love doesn't work that way! This is just loneliness! Desperation! It takes time to get to know someone! It takes time to fall in love!"

Armand slams his fist against a heavy punching bag as I debate myself. He's shouting something, like he's angry at himself, angry with the world. Soon he's punching that bag with all his strength, every muscle in his massive body flexing as he pounds it like he wants to destroy it, destroy everything, perhaps destroy himself. I can tell he's hurting. I don't know why. I don't know how. But I know what I feel.

"Give me a sign," I mutter as I feel my heart reach out to him, to this monster of a man who's fighting invisible demons right in front of me. I don't know who I'm talking to, but I say it again, that yearning to reach out to him building to breaking point. "Give me a sign."

And then, as if he hears me, Armand stops and stares through the big glass window. I freeze, wondering if he's seen me. Does he see me? Is that a sign? Am I crazy if I cross the street and walk through that door?

"Go," comes a voice from behind me, and I almost faint on my feet. Great. Now I'm hearing voices. At least this way I know for sure I'm going insane. Maybe it's my pussy talking to me.

I turn, immediately breathing a sigh of relief when I see a woman in a motorized wheelchair staring up at me with an annoyed expression.

"Go!" she says again, pointing at the flashing "Walk" sign. "Go, or step aside! You're in my way!"

I frown and look down, realizing that I'm standing on the sidewalk ramp leading to the crosswalk, blocking it with my big ass. Slowly my frown fades, and suddenly I'm smiling. I asked for a sign, didn't I? Well, here's my sign. Bright and clear. Flashing in red before my eyes.

But again my common sense pokes its nose in and whispers that I'm imagining things that aren't real, like when some nutcase swears they see a miracle just when they're looking for a miracle. It's called "Confirmation Bias" in psychology, where you see what you want to see. It's your own mind playing tricks on you. Don't do it, Astrid! Walk away!

The woman in the wheelchair yells at me again, and now the sign is flashing faster, the robotic voice calling out "Cross now! Cross now! Cross now!" with an urgency that makes me want to scream! It feels like time is running out, like I need to make my choice right here, right now! A choice that will decide my future!

"To hell with it," I whisper to myself, stepping into the street as the woman in the wheelchair curses at me. And then I'm halfway across, my head buzzing with excitement, my body tingling with a sense of anticipation, like I've really made a choice that will change everything. For both of us.

Then I'm at the door, and with a trembling hand I pull it open and step inside.

4
ARMAND

I blink in disbelief as she steps inside, past the threshold, back into my life. Then I rub my eyes, convinced that I'm hallucinating. But no, she's still here. Standing inside the doorway, feet together, lips trembling like she's nervous, like it took an immense amount of courage to come back here, to come back to me.

"Astrid," I say, the word coming out slowly. "Astrid."

"You remember my name," she says, blinking again and flashing a smile that almost breaks me. I feel vulnerable in a way I've never felt, not even when I was tied to a chair with a gun to my head. It's scary as hell. Goddamn terrifying.

"I'll never forget it," I growl, looking her up and down, taking in her strong hourglass shape that can't be hidden by the bulky sweatpants and t-shirt she's wearing. "What are you doing back here?"

"I'm asking myself the same question," she says with a forced chuckle. I can tell she's petrified, and so am I. We both know why she walked back in here. And we both know it means something. Means something in a way that defies logic and common sense.

We look into each other's eyes for what seems like forever. We don't know each other from Adam, but I know she's mine. I just know it. She's mine, and I don't give a fuck if it makes sense or not.

"Clearly you've answered the question," I say, a strange relief passing through me as I let that thought sink in: She's mine. That's all there is to it.

"I guess I have," she says softly. Then she clears her throat, breaking eye contact with me as if she's second-guessing herself, allowing some doubt to creep into her head. "Or maybe I'm crazy. Maybe I should—"

She stops mid-sentence, blinking and shaking her head as if she's losing her nerve. She's staring down at the floor, and I can see that she's a smart, practical woman who's seriously doubting why the hell she walked back in here. Her brain is butting onto the scene, whispering that she's a fool for willingly stepping back into my lair, that I'm bad news, a pervert at best, a psycho-killer at worst. And the truth is I'm both! Hah!

I feel my cock stir beneath my towel, like it's reminding me that I don't have that problem of my brain overruling my balls. I'm *all* instinct! That's what's kept me alive all these years. That sixth sense that I can't name. That sense of knowing what's around the corner, behind that locked door, hiding in the shadows. That feeling of knowing what's waiting for me, knowing what's in store for me, knowing what's mine.

Knowing what's mine.

"What am I doing?" she gasps, her voice coming out in an urgent whisper as she takes a step back away from me. She's panicking, I can tell. She's never been this bold with a man before, and it's freaking her out.

I feel two paths opening up before me, like my future is going to be decided by my next move. I can let her turn around and walk away. That's the smart thing to do. She seems like a nice girl, and there's no way in hell she's gonna be able to deal with the kind of man I am, the baggage I carry, the kind of life I'm born to lead. Again I feel that strange yearning, that need from somewhere deep inside me, the instinct of an animal to take its mate, to fill her with my seed, to see her carry my children—*our* children! This is more than just lust. It's more than the need to get my rocks off. It's something deeper than I've ever felt, something I didn't think I was capable of feeling, something I didn't believe I *deserved* to feel!

But still I stand silent, my head swirling as if I'm being pulled in a million directions at once. Astrid turns from me, hesitantly looking toward the door. I can feel the moment about to pass, like my chance for salvation is about to walk out that door, my chance for the future I want is about to leave.

"Astrid," I say, feeling like an idiot. That's all I've said to this woman so far! Her name repeated three times like a magic spell! I've never felt flustered around a woman before, never been tongue-tied like this!

"What?" she says, stopping and turning halfway, her face flush, her breathing heavy. She's flustered too, I can tell. She's freaked out by this tension that's so heavy words can't possibly cut through it.

No, I realize as I feel my confidence return in a flash of manic heat, filling my cock and my heart at the same time, unifying my body and soul in a way that feels spiritual, magical, goddamn *cosmic*. Words aren't gonna cut it here. What am I gonna say to her? "What do you do for a living? Do you have siblings? What's your favorite color? Do you like sushi?" Fuck that. I don't know shit about her, but it already feels like we're past this getting-to-know-you bullshit. Way past it.

"Stay," I say, my voice coming out in a low growl, the word coming out as a command, powered by every ounce of the man in me, the man who sees his woman. "Stay," I say again, seeing how my voice sends a shiver through her.

She turns to me, slowly, delicately, her lips trembling as if she's shocked by what she's feeling, what she's doing, what's happening. She parts those luscious red lips to say something, but then she clamps them shut again and closes her eyes like she's about to faint. I almost come again in my towel as I gaze upon her pretty round face, take in the sight of her filled-out body, breathe in the scent of her feminine musk that's like a siren calling to me in the night. It took real courage for her to walk back in here, but she's too much of a lady to just give in to what her body wants. I'm gonna need to take her there. I'm gonna need to take her.

And so I grunt away the last shreds of doubt and make my choice. Make the choice for both of us.

I kiss her.

I step forward, grab her by the arms, pull her into me, and kiss her. I kiss her hard on the lips, with everything I have. I kiss her.

By God, I kiss her.

5
ASTRID

The kiss almost breaks me, and I buckle at the knees as I feel Armand's hard body slam into mine, his strong hands close around my arms like clamps, imprisoning me and setting me free at the same time. I can't see, I can't breathe, and I sure as hell can't stop.

"Stay," he'd told me in that voice that sounded like it came from the essence of the man in him. "Astrid, stay."

That's all he's said to me, I realize as I feel his tongue push its way past my trembling lips, driving deep into my mouth like he wants to taste every inch of me, possess every inch of me, claim every inch of me. He tastes clean and warm, and I breathe deep and let his masculine aroma enter my lungs, enter my being, taking root in me like invisible claws.

Slowly I allow myself to kiss him back, and then I'm lost in him, kissing him with a hunger that brings forth my wetness in the most beautifully filthy way. I can feel my panties getting soaked through and through, and the moment Armand drops his hand down along the curve of my back and squeezes my ass, I seize up, tilt my head back, and moan out loud.

Armand grabs my ass with both hands, pulling my buttocks apart as he grinds his massive cock against my mound. He's kissing my face, my neck, my ears, marking me with his saliva like we're animals. A moment later he backs away, grabs the collar of my over-

sized T-shirt, and just rips it down the middle, yanking it off me so fast I scream in surprise.

I want to cover my boobs, but he's got me by the
wrists and he pushes me against the padded walls of
the gym, holding my arms above my head as he stares
down along my cleavage. I have a thick black sports-
bra on, but I can feel my nipples pushing against the
cloth in a way that can't be hidden.

"You're so fucking gorgeous," he groans, his mouth
opening wide as he looks down at my boobs and then
back into my eyes.

"Language," I mutter, giggling in embarrassment as
I see the need in his eyes, hear the arousal in his voice,
feel his hardness push against my slit like it wants
to force its way in through my sweats and panties!

"What're you gonna do, wash my mouth out?" he
says with a grin, placing his big hands squarely on
my breasts and squeezing so hard I scream. Then my
bra is off, and Armand's face is between my boobs,
his stubble rubbing against my soft skin and making
me squirm as he licks the valley between my rises.

I gasp and look down as he takes my left nipple
in his mouth, expertly licking my pert nub and then
biting down just enough to make me howl without
hurting me. I'm shuddering and moaning as Armand
sucks my breasts until they're both glistening in the
overhead lights of the gym. My fingers are clawing at
his short, thick hair, my back arching as I shove my
boobs into his face like I want him to take all of me
into his warm mouth.

Suddenly Armand drops to his knees, grabbing the

waistband of my sweats and pulling them smooth-
ly down past my wide hips. I gasp in shock as I look
down along my wet boobs, my shining belly, down at
Armand's face lined up with my soaked panties. I can
smell my own scent, but I'm too turned on to give a
damn. I can see the dark wet patch all along the front
of my panties, but I'm too wet to care.

"What are you doing?" I whisper, shuddering with
arousal as Armand firmly grasps my sides and pushes
me against the padded wall. He brings his face up to
my crotch, pressing his nose and mouth against the
front of my panties, breathing in deep in a way that
almost makes me come in his face. "Oh, shit, Armand!
That feels . . . it feels . . . oh, *God*!"

And then I come, my pussy spurting even as I snort
like an animal in heat. The feeling of his face against
my stiff clit is too much, and my wetness is pouring
out the sides of my panties and down my goddamn
thighs! Armand is rubbing his face into my crotch,
his hands grabbing my ass from behind as I grind into
him like a wanton woman of the night.

A moment later my panties are gone, ripped along
the seams by Armand's brutish hands and tossed halfway across the room. He jams his face back between
my thighs, parting my bare bottom with his fingers
as he parts my throbbing slit with his tongue. Then
he's fucking me with his tongue, curling it up against
the front wall of my vagina, its tip tapping against
my fibrous g-spot and making me come all over his
face in a flood of wetness.

I scream as Armand drinks from me like I'm a

fountain, his upper lip flicking my clit while his stiff tongue darts in and out of my cunt with a fury that almost destroys me. The orgasm is so intense that I'm gasping and choking as I hold on to his head and clench my pussy, clench my ass, clench every muscle in me. I can feel Armand's fingers digging into my rear crack from behind, parting my ass as I spread my thighs and come again, my climaxes rolling in like thunder, my body convulsing like I'm being struck by lightning.

Finally I collapse against the wall, the last wave of my climax hitting so hard I almost pass out. Armand lowers me to the firm floormats of the gym, and I feel secure in his strong arms, secure in a way I've never felt with anyone. He pulls me into him, kissing my forehead, stroking my hair, pressing his hips against my thighs as I finally relax and lay flat on the floor-mats, Armand covering me like a security blanket, his hard cock pressing against my mound like we were designed to fit with each other.

"What . . . was that?" I whisper, blinking probably a million times as the room slowly comes back into focus. Armand is on top of me, still stroking my hair, his eyes riveted on me like I'm some creature he's nev-er seen before. "And why are you looking at me like that? Stop it! It's making me blush!"

Armand licks his lips and flashes a devilish grin. I can see my wetness glistening on his stubble and lips like the morning dew, and I close my eyes and blush harder when I think of what just happened!

"Well, you did threaten to wash my mouth out," he

says, smacking his lips. "Hmmm. Tangy sweetness. Here. Have a taste."

"Ewww, no!" I shriek, laughing and turning my head away as Armand lowers his face to mine. But he grabs me by the hair and holds my head in place, pressing his lips against mine until I open my mouth and taste myself.

It *does* taste tangy and sweet, and I feel a fresh wave of arousal flow through me as I realize how filthy this is, how absolutely *dirty*! But it feels lighthearted and playful, and my eyes tear up when Armand props himself up on his massive arms so he can look into my eyes again. That same look. That look like . . . like I'm his.

I'm his.

The realization flashes through me like electricity, and I gasp and just nod back at him. This makes no sense, but I know I'm his. That's all there is to it. I'm his. All his. So what if we've said like three words to one another! There's no denying the depth of what just happened.

I can't speak, which is unusual for me, considering I have a career built on speaking in front of a classroom. But the words won't come. They just won't. I want to know Armand. I want to know about his life. I want to ask questions and listen to the answers. But in a way I feel like we've already answered so many questions. It's like we've skipped the getting-to-know-you nonsense of the first few dates—of the first few *months* perhaps!

"I know," he says like he can read my mind. "I feel

it too. You're mine, Astrid. I don't know how. I don't know why. But I know it. You're mine, you hear?"

I just blink up at him, nodding slightly as I wonder whether this is real, whether it *can* be real. I spend my life telling little girls not to believe in that Disney fairy-tale of their prince showing up out of the blue, and here I am falling hook, line, and sinker for the dream!

Do I dare dream it, I wonder as I feel Armand lower his head and slowly begin to kiss my neck. His warm lips send shivers through my body, and my eyes roll up in my head as I realize that I'm still wildly aroused even though I just came all over this man's face!

I reach up and touch his arms. They are thick like pillars, hard as stone, his muscles so defined that it feels like I'm touching a sculpture, a work of art. Is he really mine, I wonder as I look down past his angular face, those high cheekbones, strong jawline, thick neck. His chest is broad and magnificent, chiseled to masculine perfection, rippling with muscles that must have taken years to build up. This man isn't just strong—he's dedicated. Capable of single-minded focus. Unrelenting. Unremitting. Unstoppable.

And mine.

I frown as Armand lowers his head and begins to kiss my breasts again. Although his arms and chest are smooth and clean, I can see tattoos on his upper back. Insignias, symbols, words in some European language. Italian? I caress his arms again as he sucks my nipples, his long cock dragging past my mound and pressing against my legs, throbbing in anticipation. He wants to be inside me, I know. I want him inside me.

"What's this?" I mutter absentmindedly as I feel a rough patch on his smooth upper arm. At first I think it's a birthmark, but it feels too precise and symmetrical. Suddenly I realize it's a brand! A mark burned into Armand's flesh!

My eyes flick open as I suddenly remember those thuggish men leaving Armand's gym, remember seeing Armand pacing alone, muttering to himself, punching and hitting things as if he was a man trapped by his past, fighting for his freedom, yearning to break free. Break free from what?! Is he . . . is he a . . . a *criminal*?!

Fear whips through me even as my arousal climbs, and then suddenly Armand is back on top of me, his cock pressing against the mouth of my slit, his eyes looking deep into mine like he's asking a silent question:

Do you want this, he's asking with his eyes.

Do you want to enter my world?

Will you stand beside me, no matter what?

Will you accept me as yours, no matter what I've done, no matter what I'll do?

I reach up and touch his hard, stubbled face, look deep into his dark green eyes. Who is this man?! What has he done?! What am *I* doing?! Who the hell am *I*?!

You're his, I remind myself as I blink once as if to say yes. Whether you knew it or not, you decided you're his the moment you turned around and walked back into this place, into his life, into his arms. You're his, and that means you have to deal with whatever's coming. Now and forever.

I nod as Armand's face twists with the agony of holding his arousal back. His massive, muscled body is shivering as I touch his face with all the tenderness I have. I can tell he wants to ram himself deep into me, and my wetness is pouring down along my crack and onto the floormats as I yearn to be filled. But the moment lingers, and we just stare into one another's eyes. It's like he knows that if he enters me, it's not just his cock entering me. It's all of him. Body and soul. Mind and spirit. All of him.

And all of me.

Suddenly my eyes go into focus, my vision narrows, and all I can see are Armand's eyes, all I can feel is Armand's body, all I can smell is his aroma, the scent of a man, the scent of *my* man.

Then I close my eyes and nod once again, and Armand enters me. Enters me fully. All the way deep. Into my body. Into my soul. Into my life.

6

<u>ARMAND</u>

She's so goddamn warm against my cock that I almost explode even before I'm all the way in. I'm so hard my neck is straining, my teeth are grinding against one another, my eyes are glazed over and unfocused. I feel the arousal in every part of my flesh, and I know immediately this is more than just sex, more than just a fling, more than anything I've experienced.

This is forever.

"Oh, shit," I grunt as I push myself deep into her, feeling her open up for my thickness, her warm valley coating my shaft with its wetness until I am balls deep inside Astrid. My cock throbs as a wave of manic arousal rips through me, making my balls seize up, making my ass clench as I prepare to pump her with everything I've got. But I hold myself there for a moment, looking deep into her big brown eyes. I saw how she nodded at me—just a subtle nod, like she didn't even know she was doing it. I know what she meant. I know that nod was more than just her saying yes to my body. It was the woman in her saying yes to the man in me. To all of me. Everything I am.

Her lips tremble as she forces a smile through her arousal, and I try to smile back but I can't fucking do it. I can barely even breathe, and I wonder if I'm choking, if all the blood has left my head to fill my cock, if I'm going to die on top of her on the floor of my gym. Slowly I begin to pump, flexing my cock inside her and making her moan like the woman she is.

And then I can't hold back any longer. My body wants hers too badly, and I reach down and grasp her thick sides firmly, digging my fingers into her soft flesh, jamming my powerful hips between her thighs until she is spread wide beneath me. Then I start to pump, slowly but with power, drawing back all the way and then driving back into her, gradually picking up the pace as I grit my teeth to hold back my need. I don't want to hurt her. I never want to hurt her.

She whimpers and arches her neck back as I ram into her hard, but her body just shudders as she wraps her arms tight around my neck. Oh, fuck, she can handle me, can't she?! I knew it when I saw her! My body knew it!

With a roar I draw back and slam into her harder, gasping as I see the force of my entry vibrate her round cheeks as she shrieks. I dig my fingers deeper into her sides until I'm lifting her ass off the floor and driving into her with everything I've got. I can feel her wetness dripping down my shaft, coating my goddamn balls, flowing like a river onto the floormats. I can smell her feminine scent fill the air, fill my lungs, make me dizzy like it's a drug. She's coming, I can tell, and I shout in delight as I see her eyes roll up in her head, her tongue curling up over her upper lip.

I fuck her through her orgasm, holding her firmly by the hips as she writhes and convulses, screams and thrashes. Then I pull out of her and swiftly flip her over, raising her beautiful ass and smacking her twice on each buttcheek, watching her gorgeous rear shudder as my fingers leave streaks on her soft flesh.

"God, you're beautiful," I groan as I pull her ass higher and spread her thick thighs, rubbing her dripping slit from behind. Her scent is so strong I am grunting like an animal in heat, and I push my face into her crotch from behind and lick her from beneath, groaning again as I taste her tangy sweetness on my tongue.

She comes again as I squeeze her ass and tease her clit with my tongue, and then I raise my face, hold her slit open with my fingers, and drive my cock back into her from behind.

"Oh, *God*!" she howls as I enter her with such force that my hips slam against her rear cushion, my heavy balls swinging forward and slapping up against her underside. "Oh, God, Armand, I'm coming so hard I can't even . . . I can't even . . . oh, oh, *oh*!"

"I love you, Astrid," I mutter as I watch my glistening cock slide out from between her perfect rear buns. I drive back into her, dragging my cockhead against the walls of her vagina as I say the words again like I mean them. "I love you."

She turns her head halfway as I push all the way back into her, and I can tell she's shocked by what I just said. We both know I can't possibly mean that, but now it's out there. I've said it. Words I've never said to any woman. Not one. Not a single one.

Astrid turns her head away from me and arches her back, spreading her thighs and bracing herself as I drive into her again. Her strong hourglass shape is a vision of beauty laid out before me, her love handles perfectly sized for my meaty paws, her ass designed to take the power of my push. I wonder if she heard what I said, and even through my arousal I feel a strange vulnerability, like I've exposed myself to this woman, let her inside me even as I drive deep inside her! This woman could hurt me, I realize as that shock mounts even as my climax approaches, my balls begin to seize up in preparation to fill Astrid, fill her until she overflows. She could break me.

"Astrid," I mutter as I get closer, closer to orgasm, closer to madness perhaps. "Astrid, listen, I . . ."

"I love you too," she whispers, turning her head to the side again so I can see her pretty face in profile. "I love you too, Armand."

And then she lowers her head again, looks down past her hanging boobs, and reaches one hand for my balls. She cups them delicately, massaging them gently, her motion somehow in rhythm with my furious thrusts. It feels like a perfect union. Her gentleness and my power. Her curves and my ridges.

Her womb and my seed.

The thought pierces me like a knife, and I seize up when I realize what's about to happen, what I know is going to happen like I can see it written in the stars, in our future, in the book of life itself.

And then it all comes together. My past. My future. My woman. My destiny.

I ram back into her one last time as Astrid clutches my balls and holds me inside her. Then I roar and arch my neck back, feeling every muscle in my body go rigid as my climax hits with the force of a freight train blasting off the tracks. My cock flexes so hard inside her I can feel it push against her inner walls, and the first shot of my load is so explosive I almost pass out.

I know I'm shouting at the top of my lungs, but I can't hear a fucking thing as I pour my semen into Astrid like I've been saving it my entire life for this moment. She's screaming too, but all I hear is beautiful silence, the music of the universe, nothing but our heartbeats sounding out like drums in the night.

I come for what seems like hours, and then I clench my balls and deliver the last of my load, give her everything I have. A moment later I collapse on top of her, pressing her flat onto the floormat with my heavy body, hearing her groan and then sigh as I cover her like a blanket.

She's mine, I think as I feel us breathe heavily, in perfect rhythm with each other. She's mine. Now and forever. I'll love her. Protect her. Kill for her. Fucking *die* for her. She's mine, and I'm never letting go, no matter what comes in the way.

7
ASTRID

Oh, shit, he's coming inside me, I think in panic as I feel Armand's cock flex against my inner walls and then blast a volley of his semen so far up my vagina I swear I can taste it in my throat. I'm cupping his balls with my right hand, barely even realizing what I'm doing until I feel them seize up as they deliver massive volumes of semen through his spurting cock, filling me until I'm overflowing down my goddamn thighs!

But my pussy clenches around his cock, squeezing and releasing like it's milking him, and I know that fleeting sense of panic was the last bit of the woman I used to be going up in smoke. I've barely had sex in my life, let alone unprotected sex, but here I am holding a tattooed man's balls, my pussy milking him dry, my valley filled and overflowing with his seed!

A smile breaks on my face as I hear Armand shout like he can't control himself, like he's all animal, all beast, all power and fury. My body is throbbing from the pounding I've just taken, but it feels so damned good that I scream in delight. I'm still holding his balls, gently massaging them as he flails against my ass, pushing out load after load of his thick semen like he's been saving it for me, just for me, only for me.

I know I'm coming, but I've been coming so hard and for so long that it just feels like a continuous orgasm, like my climaxes have all burst over the edge like a waterfall and are now flowing together like a mighty river, sweeping me along with it. I scream, but I can barely hear myself over the pounding blood between my temples, the frantic drumbeat of my heart, the rush of ecstasy in my body as I come again as Armand fills me until I overflow.

With a mighty roar he finishes, collapsing on top of me and pushing me down face-first onto the firm floor-mats which are sticky from our heat. His weight feels wonderful on me, and I sigh and groan as he smothers me like a blanket, his big body easily covering me, holding me, protecting me.

Claiming me.

His cock is still inside me as we lay there in silence, and I feel him still oozing into me. We are both hot and wet, sticky with each other's natural oils, and I sigh again as I hear his heart beat against my back. It takes a moment for me to realize it, but then I notice that our hearts are beating in time, in perfect rhythm, absolute synchronicity. It's probably just my mind playing tricks on me—perhaps my body playing tricks on me. But in the moment it feels like the perfect ending to what just happened.

"What just happened?" I whisper, turning my head as Armand kisses my cheek from behind and then slowly rolls off me. I turn on my side, and he cradles me in his big arms, looking deep into my eyes, his big jaw wide with a smile.

"We did," he says without hesitation. "*We* just happened, Astrid."

The sound of my name rolling off his tongue makes

me shiver, and I burrow into him, marveling at how small I feel against his massive frame. I am not a small woman. I've never been a small woman. But with him I feel light as a feather, graceful as a butterfly, beautiful as a beach sunset.

"Armand," I say slowly, realizing that this could be the first time I'm actually speaking his name out loud! "Is that Italian?"

"It's marketing, is what it is," he says with a chuckle. Then he raises an eyebrow and deepens his voice. "*Belisimo, mon cheri!*"

"That's not a very good Italian accent," I say with a snort. "You'd never make it in the mafia."

His face darkens, his eyes clouding over, his jaw tightening as I almost kick myself for what I just said. But then a chill goes through me as I think back to those slick goons who'd visited Armand before I walked back through that door . . . walked back and spread my legs for him!

Now that panic comes back with a vengeance, and my heart almost stops as everything feels too much, just too goddamn much! OMG, I just slept with a man about whom I know nothing! He came inside me! What if I—

"I never did make it in the mafia," Armand says, blinking and focusing on me. "I was always the outsider. The man in the shadows. It suited me well enough. Allowed me to get out clean."

He pauses at the last word, and I blink as I look up at him. "Um, did you just tell me that you were in the mafia?" I say with a trembling breath, searching his face to see if he's messing with me. "I was just kidding, you know."

"You weren't kidding," he says quietly like he knows me. "And neither was I."

I blink again, a shiver going through me as Armand cups my ass and pulls me close, nuzzling into my hair. His scent is strong—clean and masculine. I love it. I want to take in his smell with every breath. Forever.

"I killed for them," he says after that pause, his voice wavering subtly, like it took deliberate effort for him to say that.

"Sorry, what?" I whisper, blinking as I wonder if I'm dreaming. "I don't think I heard you right."

"You heard me just fine," he says, his eyes narrowing to dark slits. But he doesn't scare me. He couldn't scare me. I feel safe with him. I *shouldn't* feel safe with him—after all, he's three times my size and just told me he's a . . . a . . .

"You're messing with me," I say, shaking my head and forcing a smile. "Mafia hitman? Really? And now you're the owner of *Body by Armand*? You in witness protection? Is the FBI watching us right now? Ohmygod, my big ass is going on record with the Federal Government?!"

Armand chuckles, placing both hands on my buttcheeks and squeezing tight. "I've got you covered. Your modesty is secure with me."

"Modesty? Um, I don't think I have any left!" I say, feeling my face go flush as I think back to the wildness of what we just did.

"Yes, you do. I know it took courage to walk back

in here. You were scared out of your mind, but you did it anyway."

"That's stupidity, not courage," I say, glancing down as I see the admiration in his eyes. "And certainly not modesty." I blink and look past Armand's shoulder. "Speaking of modesty though, where are my clothes. Oh, that's right. They're ripped to shreds. How the hell am I going to get home?!"

"You *are* home," he says, still holding me, the seriousness in his voice making me swoon. But reality is knocking at the door somewhere in my head, and I swallow hard as I try to make sense of my life—my life which seems to have taken a very sharp left turn.

"So we're going to live here, in a gym, naked on blue floormats?" I say, refusing to accept what he truly meant—that *he* was my home, my man, my forever.

Armand shrugs against me. "Where would you like to live, Astrid?"

I scrunch my face up and raise an eyebrow. "Costa Rica, perhaps?"

He snorts. "Costa Rica? Where did that come from?"

I chuckle, feeling my body relax again as I snuggle into him. "The girls were talking about it the other day."

Armand frowns, a shadow passing across his face. "You have kids? How many?"

Wait, is he jealous? For some reason his possessiveness makes me feel warm inside, and I just shrug and look up like I'm counting. "Twenty-three," I say.

Armand stares, cocking his head like now *he's* counting!

"Ohmygod, do you really believe I've popped out twenty-three kids in my lifetime!" I say with mock indignation. "I'm not *that* old! Or am I just so fat you assume I've popped out quadruplets every year?!"

Armand frowns and smacks me on the bottom, making me yelp from the sting of his open palm. "We don't use the word fat in this place," he says sternly. "At least not in a negative sense. Fat is the body's preferred fuel, you know. A healthy body would much rather use fat instead of sugar for energy."

I bite my lip and raise an eyebrow. "Um, well, I like sugar too. Sorry."

He grunts and kisses me hard on the lips, pushing his tongue into my mouth and swirling it around as I gasp. "That explains why you taste so sweet," he says, pulling away and licking his lips.

I snort and shake my head, which is dizzy from the kiss. "It doesn't explain why your jokes are so lame," I retort.

"Careful," he says, smacking me gently on the ass again before digging his fingers into my side. "You might hurt my feelings."

"Oooh, a sensitive mafia hitman?" I say. "The complete package!"

Armand loses the smile, but his gaze holds steady. "I don't have any regrets. I was a soldier. A soldier does his duty. Does what he's been asked to do. What he's been paid to do."

I frown, that chill going through me again as I slowly start to believe him. I'm silent as I swallow hard, my breath catching as I slowly acknowledge that the chill running through my body is excitement, not fear. It's a sense of thrill, not disgust!

I study Armand's face, taking in every tiny scar on his high cheekbones, every line on his forehead, those wrinkles of experience around his devastatingly sincere eyes. I can tell he's made a conscious choice to open up to me, to expose himself, to take the risk that I'll call him a monster, scream and run away from him.

Why *aren't* I screaming and running the hell away, I ask myself as I tenderly caress his rough stubble, look deep into his eyes. I know the answer, but I can't admit it to myself. I'm not ready to admit it. I'm not ready to accept that I'm truly willing to accept this man for who he is—*whatever* he is. Ohmygod, am I one of those nutcase women who write love letters to serial killers in prison?!

"You're a good man," I say, my words coming out with a confidence that surprises me. I know I'm right. I see it in his eyes. I feel it in his touch. I know it sounds cheesy, but I say it anyway. I say it again. "You're a good man, Armand."

He flashes me a look that for the first time sparks fear in me, and I realize I've touched a nerve. I remind myself I know nothing about him, and I blink and gasp as I feel his body tense up against mine.

"I'm trying," he says after a long, shuddering breath. Then that look is gone from his eyes, like he's just flipped a switch with the sheer power of his will. Is that the willpower it takes to be a killer, I wonder. The ability to turn off just like that, to control your emotions like you're just a machine? "How about you?" he says with a grin. "Are you a good woman, Astrid? Been good all your life?"

I blink, suddenly feeling the spotlight turn to me. Not that I'm uncomfortable in the spotlight—after all, I stand up in front of a class of judgmental nine-year-olds every day!

"No," I say softly, blushing like a schoolgirl even though it's completely unlike me. Well, unlike the person I want to be, at least. The person I chose to be years ago. I chose to be confident even though I was ashamed of my body. I chose to be outgoing, even though a part of me wanted to curl up at home and hide from the world. I chose to be all those things. They were good choices. So why does Armand's question make me uncomfortable? "No," I say again.

He snorts, his dark green eyes narrowing as he scans my face. "Liar," he whispers. "You've always been a good girl, haven't you? Volunteering at the animal shelter. Spending Christmas at the soup kitchen. Helping little old ladies cross the street."

I laugh, thinking back to that woman in a wheelchair who cursed me as I stood there across the street outside Armand's door, debating on whether to cross.

"Stop teasing me," I say. "You make it sound like doing all those things are lame!"

"Ah, so you *did* do all those things!" he says in triumph. "Little Astrid the goody-goody girl scout! Damn, I'm good at figuring out people."

I laugh and shake my head. "Let's not get ahead of ourselves." I puff out my cheeks and sigh pointedly. "Wrong on all counts."

He frowns and closes one eye. "I find that hard to believe."

"Believe what you want," I say. "But here's the truth: I was allergic to animals as a kid, so no pet shelter. I actually did volunteer at a soup kitchen once, but I was kicked out for stuffing my own face while serving the homeless. As for helping old ladies cross the street . . . well, there's probably a woman in a wheelchair who will strongly disagree with that."

Armand's eyes widen and he laughs out loud, pulling me close and giving me a big sloppy kiss like we've known each other for years. "Hah!" he roars. "You got fired from a volunteer job?! That's ridiculous!"

"I know!" I say, laughing along with him as I blush. I don't think I've told anyone about that. "But I was hungry, and there was all this food laid out on the serving line! All I did was eat a muffin! They made it seem like I was stealing or something!"

"Bastards," Armand says, tightening his jaw and pretending to be angry. "I'll kill them all!"

I almost spit in his face as I burst out laughing. "You'll kill the hungry homeless and the people who volunteer to feed them? All for me? That's *so* romantic, Armand!"

He shrugs and grunts. "Yeah, well, you *did* say I was a good man. A good man takes care of his woman."

A warmth rolls through me as I feel Armand cradle

me like I'm his, and I feel the truth of his words even though it doesn't make sense. "Oh, I'm your woman now?" I say, trying to make it sound lighthearted as my heart feels like it's about to pop out from between my boobs and do a little dance on the blue floormats!

"You are," he says without hesitation. His tone isn't lighthearted at all. He's serious. Dead serious. "You have a problem with that, Astrid?"

I blink, trying to fight my instinct to just submit to him, to give in, to whisper, *Yes, of course I'm yours!* It's too soon, I tell myself in my stern, teacher-voice. How can you be a role model for young girls if you just give yourself to a man after spending an hour with him!

"Society might have a problem with that," I say.

"Fuck society," he growls against my hair, pulling me closer, his hands rubbing my naked ass, his cock thickening against my soft thighs.

"Language," I mutter, feeling my own heat rise again as Armand runs his big hand along my rear crack, pulling my buttcheeks apart and then letting go. "Oh, Armand. That feels good. That feels . . . oh, oh . . ."

"Say it," he whispers as he spreads my rear cheeks again, this time holding them wide apart and running the thick fingers of one hand lengthwise along my rear crack. "Say it, good little Astrid. Let that bad girl come out. Come out just for me. Only for me."

"For you," I gurgle as my heat ratchets up and my wetness flows afresh. I can still feel Armand's seed inside me, and the thought of him putting more inside me makes me so hot I almost come! What's happening to me?! What is he doing to me?! What is he bringing out in me?!

"Astrid's been a bad girl, hasn't she?" Armand whispers as he kisses my lips and fingers my rear hole in a way that's so filthy I choke and shudder with arousal.

"Yes," I whisper, my tongue curling up over my lip on its own as Armand kisses my neck, my boobs, sucking each nipple until my nubs are hard and pointy again. I close my eyes and let his words sink in. I think about how I crossed that street, walked through this door, spread my legs for a man I barely know. A man who now says I'm his. His woman. His girl. His *bad* girl.

Feelings I didn't know I had rise up in me as Armand moves down along my curves, firmly caressing my sides and then gripping my hips tight and flipping me over. I can sense his need, the needs of a man, a hard man, a rough man, a man who's done things that society would shake its head at and say, "Tsk. Tsk."

Fuck society, I think as Armand pulls my ass up and spreads my thighs, groaning from behind me as I feel his cock spring to full hardness, its massive shaft slapping up against my mound from beneath. Slowly he spreads my rear cheeks, and I can feel his eyes taking in the view of the dark space of my crack. I want to be embarrassed. I want to feel ashamed. But I'm not. This man is bringing out a different side of me, a side I don't want to admit I have, a side that society doesn't want to admit women have.

The need to be claimed by a man.

The need to be taken by a man.

The need to be dominated by a man.

I gasp as Armand brings his right palm down firmly on my asscheek, making my body seize up from the shock. He holds his hand against my buttcheek for a moment, slowly rubbing my ass as the stinging subsides. Then he spanks the other cheek, making my ass shudder as I gasp again. The slaps were firm but not hard. Not yet.

"What are you doing?" I gurgle, feeling the blood rush to my face as he massages my ass.

He doesn't reply, and when I turn my head halfway and catch sight of his expression, I almost choke at the sight of how goddamn aroused he is! In that moment I understand who Armand is, what he needs, what he wants. And I know I want to give it to him. Give him what he needs. Give him *everything* he needs. Every part of me.

He blinks as he sees me looking at him, and then suddenly he lets go of my ass, his jaw tightening as if he's struggling to gain control of himself . . . gain control before he loses control.

"I'm sorry," he growls, shaking his head and going back on his knees. "You aren't ready for this. Did I hurt you?"

I turn on my side and glance at him. He's sitting back on his knees, his cock standing straight up in the air like a post, thick with the blood of his arousal, heavy with the force of his need. Yet he's holding

himself back. The power of his will overruling the
need of his body.

I feel a tingling between my legs, and I imagine
his thick shaft entering me from behind. I've never even come close to being taken that way. Hell, I'd
have slapped any guy who even suggested it! But the
few guys I've been with haven't made me feel the way
Armand makes me feel. They haven't brought out
the woman in me like he has. They haven't made me
want to . . . to submit.

"You couldn't hurt me if you tried," I say softly even
as my ass stings from the way he spanked me. The
words sound ridiculous as I take in the sight of Armand's massive body, muscles glistening with sweat
under the yellow overhead lights. That cock is still
standing upright, and I gulp as I imagine myself being
stretched wide and entered from behind! Um, yeah,
that would probably hurt. Maybe he's right. Maybe
I'm *not* ready for this. Not ready for him.

Armand smiles gently, reaching out and touching
my face. He pulls me against his hard body, smoth-
ering me with a protective hug. I feel small next to
him. I've never felt small in my life. Never felt pro-
tected like this. Never felt safe like this.

"You're clueless, aren't you?" he says softly. "You
think I'm a good man? That I couldn't hurt you if I
tried? Oh, Astrid. I should walk away before . . . before I . . . before we . . ."

"Fine," I say, nuzzling up against his massive chest.
I don't believe him for a moment. He's not walking

away. I just know he's not. I'm his woman. He said so. "Walk away then. Goodbye."

He snorts with laughter, leaning down and kissing me on the head. His big hand moves down to my rump and he cups my ass and squeezes. "Actually, this is my gym. It would be kinda dumb for me to walk away."

"Oh, so you're kicking me out?" I whisper, looking up at him and raising an eyebrow. "Wham, bam, thank you Ma'am?"

"I don't recall saying thank you," he growls down at me, a cocky smile breaking on his dark red lips, his green eyes dancing with mischief. "And what exactly do you mean by wham-bam? Are you implying that I have a quick trigger?"

I laugh against his chest. "Quick is an understatement. Do you remember what happened when you opened the door for me the first time?"

His tanned face goes red and he snorts again. "Shit, you noticed that?" He squeezes my ass again. "It's your fault for showing up on my doorstep, boobs jiggling, ass bouncing, those painted lips whispering Fuck Me with every breath!"

I squeal with surprise, pushing against him to break away. "Ohmygod!" I shout, trying to control my laughter. "You are such a pig! I was wearing the most non-flattering clothes I own—and I own a lot of nonflattering clothes! As for lipstick—that was Vaseline!"

"Hmmm, Vaseline," Armand growls, yanking me back towards him, his big hands spreading my buttcheeks, his finger shamelessly circling my rear pucker in a way that makes me gasp.

"You are *sick*!" I whisper as the arousal whips through me again. Armand is still hard against me, his cock pressed between our bodies, his length reaching all the way up past my belly-button! "That is *not* happening. It's just not physically possible."

"I'll decide what's physically possible," he mutters, still circling my rear hole.

"Is that what Body by Armand means on the sign outside?" I say.

"Actually, I'm gonna change it to Body *for* Armand," he retorts. "And now you're going to be my only client."

"I'm flattered," I say. "Though LuAnn will be disappointed that she'll have to find another butt-doctor to help keep her marriage alive."

"LuAnn . . ." he says. "Oh, right. Older lady. You guys friends?"

"LuAnn's my principal. She gave me a gift certificate for this place."

"Principal? Like a school principal?"

"Yes," I say, remembering that we've only just met and we still don't know anything about each other even though it feels like we know *everything*!

"You still in school?" he says, patting my butt gently. "Do I need your parents' permission before I make you mine?"

I laugh. "Little late for that, isn't it?" I laugh again. "No, I'm a teacher, silly! Fourth grade."

"So your school principal gave you a gift certificate to a gym? That's a bit unusual."

I shrug. "I guess she thought my ass was too flabby."

Armand squeezes my ass again. "It's perfect," he whispers, his cock throbbing against me like it agrees. "Perfect for me. Your principal doesn't know what she's talking about. I'm going to ban her from my gym for body-shaming."

"She means well," I say. "She wants her teachers to be happy in their personal lives. She thinks it makes them better teachers." I pause and nod. "I agree with her. Being a teacher is more than a job. Those girls look up to me. They're influenced by my mood, by how I conduct myself, by the person I am. The woman I am."

"What would they say if they saw Ms. Astrid now?" Armand whispers.

I giggle. "They'd say I was being bad."

Armand grunts. "And what happens to bad girls, Astrid?" he whispers, massaging my ass with increasing force.

"I . . . I don't know," I stammer as my arousal takes my breath away, leaving me gasping against him. "What happens to bad girls?"

"They get disciplined," he whispers. "They get tied up and spanked by teacher."

I snort, my eyes going wide. "Um, what world are you living in? Besides, I'm the teacher here!"

"Not in my house, you aren't. In here, I'm the teacher. I'm the trainer. I'm in charge. You understand?"

"Oh, really? So you're going to teach me to be a good girl?"

"No," he whispers, smacking my butt tight and then grabbing my arms and turning me around so I'm facing away from him, staring directly at the floor-to-ceiling mirror that covers one wall of the gym. I stare at myself, the arousal whipping through me like a snake as I see myself naked, my boobs hanging off to either side, my dark triangle wet and matted, Armand's thick semen all over my pubic curls.

"No," Armand whispers against my neck, and I gasp as I see his big hands reach around me and press my boobs so hard it hurts. "I'm going to teach you to be bad. I'm going to teach you to be mine. All mine. Now look at yourself, Astrid. Look at yourself."

8
<u>ARMAND</u>

"**L**ook at yourself, Astrid," I whisper as I press my cock against her lower back. My arousal is back with a vengeance, and I know this time I'm not going to be able to stop myself. I need to possess her completely. Make her mine in a way I've never done with any woman. Own her from the inside out. She's mine, and she needs to know it. The fucking world needs to know it.

Astrid blinks as she looks at her own reflection and then at my reflection. I pinch her nipples hard, plucking at her dark red nubs until they are erect and pointy. Then I cup her tits from beneath and hold them up so she can see herself.

"Look at yourself," I say again, reaching up with one hand and gently rubbing her neck. Slowly I grip her chin and turn her head so she's forced to look straight ahead. "Look at us."

Astrid looks at our reflection, blinking with self-consciousness as she sees my gaze move all along her curves, taking in the sight of her beautiful breasts, her wide hips, her thick thighs. I can tell Astrid is a woman who's accepted her own body for what it is, but like many larger women she's still not sure if a man will accept her body as it is, as it's meant to be, as *his*.

"Every body has its own natural shape, and that natural shape is perfection. It's the very *definition* of perfection," I say softly, running my free hand along her hourglass curves. "Just like every flower has its own shape, its own pattern, its own beauty. A flower doesn't fight its shape. It understands that it's been designed that way by nature, designed just right."

"Designed for what?" she whispers, blinking as she meets my gaze.

Slowly I move out from behind her, kneeling beside her and sliding my arm around her sturdy waist until we're side by side like in a portrait. A portrait of love.

I glance down at my cock, which is ramrod straight, thick as a goddamn redwood, its heavy tip swollen and oozing with fresh precum. I can see Astrid's slit peeking out through her dark feminine curls. She really does look like a flower in full bloom, opened up for the rain. Opened up for me. Just me. Always me.

"Designed for each other," I whisper as my arousal soars to a level that feels beyond just the physical. And then suddenly everything snaps into focus, like I know what has to happen, what needs to happen, what's designed to happen!

I'm already on my knees, and so I just turn to her, grasping her by the hips and turning her to face me. From the corner of my vision I can see the two of us in profile, and I can feel the universe looking down on us like it approves of what I'm about to do. Maybe I've lost my fucking mind, I tell myself as I feel the words forming on my lips. Hell, of *course* I've lost my mind! Lost it in her.

"Will you marry me?" I say, the words almost making me choke as my heart hammers inside my chest. "Astrid, will you marry me?"

She stares into my eyes, her mouth hanging open, her breath catching. "Armand . . ." she begins to say. "Armand, I . . . I . . ."

But she can't finish the sentence, because suddenly the front door crashes open, tinted glass shattering, splinters of wood shooting all over as Gustav's goons swarm into my gym!

"No!" I roar, my instincts taking over as I immediately realize I'm outnumbered, that I can't get to my gun in time, that trying to fight these men will just get me shot down. And so I just spread my arms out wide and shield Astrid, backing up against the mirror and pushing her flat against it to preserve her modesty.

"Relax, Armand," says Number One even though from the way he's pointing his gun at me he's anything but relaxed. "Gustav just wants to talk."

"Turn around and walk away and maybe I won't kill you all when this is over," I growl through gritted teeth. "Actually, you know what? I'm lying. You guys are all gonna fucking die. All I can promise is that I'll do it quick."

"Hey, we're just following orders," says Number Two, blinking as he sees how serious I am. "Like he said, Gustav just wants to talk."

"You coulda told me that when you walked in an hour ago!" I thunder. "Instead of smashing through my door like fucking psychos!"

"Yeah, well, things changed in the past hour," says

Number One. He turns and nods at Number Two. "Toss them some clothes, will ya? I've seen enough of Armand's ass today to last me a lifetime."

Number Two looks around before seeing the shelf of gym clothes for sale behind the counter. He grabs a pile of trackpants and sweatshirts and flings them over to me. I grab them and hand Astrid a set, kneeling square in front of her as she hurriedly puts them on behind me. Then I stand up and slowly dress myself, taking my time so I can assess the situation.

I believe Number One when he says something changed over the past hour. No way these guys would have paid me a courtesy visit and then come blasting through my door an hour later!

"All right," I say when I'm dressed and my breathing is under control, my instincts on high alert. I've got four loaded guns pointing at me, and although if I were alone I might try something, I can't risk Astrid taking a bullet. "All right," I say again, holding my arms out to the side, palms open. "I'll talk to Gus. But she's got no part in this. Let her go, and I'll come quietly."

"You'll come quietly either way," Number One says. "Both of you."

A chill comes over me when I see Number One's hand tremble. Clearly he's rattled. That's not a good sign. If he's rattled, it means Gustav's rattled. And when Gustav gets rattled, people die. Sometimes a lot of people.

Darkness wafts over me as I realize there's no way they're letting Astrid walk away. Not after she's seen these guys, heard the name Gustav. The old man is paranoid about witnesses. Hell, in twenty years of killing for Gus, he's never directly given me a kill-order! It's always been through one of his guys. Always a degree of separation, just in case I end up on a witness stand someday. Is the old man losing it? Cleaning house? Is the law catching up to him?

Only one way to find out, I think as I take a deep breath and come to terms with the fact that I'm going with these guys, going to the lion's den.

And Astrid's coming with me.

Despair reaches up through me like a living beast, choking me from the inside as I want to kick myself for letting that woman walk through this door! There's a reason I never let anyone get close to me over the years! Nobody has ever had leverage over me. No family. No friends. No woman I ever gave a shit about. I was my own man, and suddenly I'm not! Suddenly I'm vulnerable! Suddenly I have a weakness!

"You guys ready?" says Number One, gesturing with his gun toward the door.

I close my eyes and shake my head, taking deep breaths as I feel my world falling apart. I'm about to snarl out a reply to this asshole, but I stop cold when I hear Astrid speak from behind me.

"Yes," she says, her voice trembling but in a way that makes me turn and stare at her.

"Yes," she says again. But she isn't looking at Number One. She isn't looking at the guns pointed at us. She's looking at me. Into my eyes. Into my soul.

And my heart almost stops when I realize that she isn't answering Number One's question.

She's answering my question.

And suddenly that darkness is blasted away by a feeling of love so overwhelming that I can barely speak. There are four gunmen in the room, but I don't give a shit anymore. They can shoot me in the back if they want. I can die now, because my life feels complete.

With a roar I pull Astrid into me, hugging her so hard I feel the air pushed out of her so fast she gasps.

Yes, I'll marry you, is what she just said to me! Yes, I'll marry you!

And now that sense of despair is replaced with a beacon of hope. Now I understand that this woman just made a bold choice, a choice to stand beside me no matter what, even if it means we're lying beside each other in an unmarked grave by tomorrow morning! She doesn't make me weak, I realize with shocked delight. She makes me stronger! That's what a woman does for her man, isn't it?! She makes him *more* of a man, not less!

She makes him a complete man.

9
<u>ARMAND</u>

"The man is dead," says Gustav, running his hand through his thinning hair in a way that I can tell means he's nervous. "Murdered in his bed. An inside job."

I frown as I look at the old man sitting in his high-backed wooden chair. He looks smaller than I remember. More shriveled. But his eyes are gray and focused like a wolf's. Sharp and piercing like the ruthless mob boss he is. He's not losing it, I decide. But that only means that if he's this rattled, something big is up.

"What man?" I say, scanning the massive open room in Gus's lakeside bungalow on the outskirts of town. There isn't much furniture in here. Gus was always on his feet, always walking, always on the move. I liked that about him. Sitting is murder on the body.

"Mory Michaels," Gus says, grinding his teeth as he runs his hand through his hair once more.

I frown again, but this time because I suddenly understand why Gus is so freaked out. Mory Michaels is a rival mob boss. Secretive. Reclusive. Totally behind the scenes. He and Gus go way back. Rumor has it they'd come to an agreement decades ago, after a brutal mob war had decimated both sides and got the Feds probing into what the hell was going on in our town. They'd declared a truce, divided up territory, and shaken hands on it. This was back in a time when a handshake between men meant something. That's another thing I always liked about Gus. His word meant something.

I swallow hard as I put the pieces together. I'm not like one of Gus's soldiers—not really. I'm an independent contractor, and Gus always respected that.

"Sorry to hear that, I guess," I say in a deadpan tone. "But that doesn't explain why you sent your goons to smash through my door when you coulda just knocked. I thought you were civilized, Gus."

"Drastic times call for drastic measures, Armand," says Gus, his teeth still gnashing.

"Sounds like your problem, not mine," I say.

Gus glances at Astrid with his gray wolf-eyes, that one look telling me everything I need to know. My body stiffens as I decide I'm going to kill everyone in this room. Simple as that. You don't threaten my woman. You don't threaten my . . . fiancée?!

I blink as I remember that I only just met this woman, and now we're engaged! Maybe we'll be dead by tonight! All of life's major events compressed into twenty-four hours! A lifetime in one fucking day!

But I feel my heart twist as images of Astrid round and pregnant, her belly swollen with my babies pushes its way into my mind. We aren't going to die today. We have so much more to do together. I know it. I feel it. And I will have it. I'll have that future with Astrid, and I don't care what I have to do to get it.

"What do you want, Gus? Another hit? Sure. Give me a name and it's done. It's done, and then I'm done.

We're done. One more and you leave me alone. You leave *us* alone."

Gus narrows his eyes, his lips tightening into something between a smile and a grimace. He gives me this half-shrug, half-nod, like he's saying sure, you got it. But he still hasn't said a word. What's he hiding?

"Do I have your word?" I say, my jaw clenching as I hold Gus's gaze.

Gus sighs and looks down for a moment. "My word isn't the problem," he says grimly. "It's your word that's the issue here."

I frown as I see something in Gus's eyes that reminds me that the old man has always been a man of honor, that even though he'd chosen a life of crime, he still had morals. His business was money-lending and protection, in a way no different from what a bank or a private security firm might do. He never lost his way by dealing killer drugs or doing something vile like human trafficking.

Yeah, Gus had morals and so do I, I think as I cock my head and try to figure out why Gus had me dragged here at gunpoint instead of just asking me nicely. I have lines I don't cross, lines I never crossed as a killer. I was cold-blooded, but I never took pleasure in spilling another man's blood. I never killed anybody who didn't have it coming, and Gus knew better than to even ask.

Which means that if he didn't ask this time, it's because he knew I'd say no.

"You asking me to kill an innocent man?" I say in a whisper. "Someone who doesn't have it coming?"

"Oh, this person has it coming," Gus says, rubbing his gray stubble. He turns to Astrid, smiling tightly as he looks her dead on. "What would you say about a woman who poisons her husband so she can take over his empire?"

I stare at Gus as he looks back at me. "A woman?" I say, feeling my throat tighten. "I've never killed a woman, Gus. I don't kill women. No innocent men. No kids. And no goddamn women!"

Gus closes his eyes and sighs, shaking his head slowly. When he opens his eyes, his gaze darts back to Astrid and then to me again. "And I've always respected that line for you, Armand. However I have no choice here. Which means *you* have no choice either."

"There's always a choice," I snap back at Gustav, that protective instinct taking me close to losing my shit and leaping across the room. I'd snap this geezer's neck before his gunmen can pump enough lead into me to slow me down. "You've got a fucking army at your disposal, Gus! Why me?!"

Gus shakes his head. "Thirty years ago I shook the hand of Mory Michaels and promised him a truce."

"Well, Mory's dead now, which means you aren't bound by that promise."

Gus snorts. "You know me better than that, Armand." He shakes his head again. "It means I'm bound forever by that promise. I will never break the truce first, which means I can't send in my army, guns blazing. I need an outsider. An independent. A man who's lived his life in the shadows. It has to be you, Armand. I cannot allow this woman to take over Mory's empire."

"Why not?" I say with a shrug. "As long as she keeps the truce, stays to her territory, minds her own business, what do you care? Live and let live, Gus! Lighten up, buddy!"

"There's no light in this woman, Armand," says Gus, his voice dropping to a whisper. "Mory was the only one holding her in check all these years. Now he's gone, and God help the children if she takes the reins."

I shake my head as if to clear it. Maybe old Gus *has* lost it. "God help the *children*? What the fuck are you talking about, Gus?"

"Something so vile it sickens even a cold bastard like myself," says Gus. "Armand, this woman has built a career that gives her access to children. Young children. Young girls."

I almost choke as I try to process what Gus is telling me. "You're insane," I mutter, shaking my head. I turn to Astrid and roll my eyes. "We're leaving, Astrid. Old man's lost it."

"No, wait," she says, her eyes focused on Gus like she's actually believing the shit he's spouting. "I want to hear this."

"No, you don't," I say, grabbing her arm and trying to pull her towards me. Gus might be losing it, but he's still a man of honor. He's not going to fucking execute us. And torturing a loved one to get me to do something isn't his style either. Those threatening glances towards Astrid was a bluff. Gustav's always been good at that. I almost fell for it, but I know better now. This is his problem, not mine.

"Yes, I do!" Astrid snaps, pulling away from me and taking three steps towards Gus as every gun in the room points towards her. She stops in her tracks, but her face is peaked, her eyes shining with determination, her soft body tensed up with strength that I can see flowing through her! It's fucking exhilarating, and I stand there and stare at my woman in astonishment. "Children are my life, Armand. I need to know what he means!"

Gus leans forward on his chair, his face lighting up with what I know is admiration. He narrows his eyes, like he's wondering if he can trust her. Then he nods, takes a breath, and leans back in his chair.

"You have children?" he says softly.

Astrid shakes her head. Then she flicks a glance over at me before focusing on Gus again. "Not yet," she says, and I tighten when I see how her right hand cups her rounded belly involuntarily, like she knows my seed is inside her already. "But I'm a teacher. I've had a hand in raising hundreds of girls over the years. I need to know what you're talking about."

Gus frowns, rubbing his stubble. "A teacher? Where?"

"St. Francis for Girls," she says.

Gus's jaw drops so fast I think he might die in his chair, and I swear he gasps so loud I think he's choking. Much as I respect the man, I'm not giving him mouth to mouth. Let Number One do it.

But Gus isn't dying. He's chuckling, shaking his head as he coughs and sputters. "Do you two believe in fate?" he asks, still shaking his head as his smile widens.

I raise an eyebrow and think about everything that's happened over the past day. I've never been particularly spiritual, but I have noticed certain patterns in my own life that seemed like it was part of a plan: coincidences, strokes of luck, sometimes events that defied probability, like there was someone watching out for me in all those dangerous situations I got myself into. Like I was being pulled along a certain path.

"Yes, I believe in fate," says Astrid, turning and flashing me another quick look.

"How about you, Armand?" says Gus.

"Just spit it out, old man," I growl, refusing to answer. "What you got? What's making you smile like a crazy old fart?"

"Destiny," says Gus with a twinkle in his eye. He winks at me and shrugs. "Looks like you won't need to betray your morals after all, Armand. Because your woman is going to take care of things. All's well that ends well. A perfect ending. Happily ever after for all of us!" He takes a breath and turns back to Astrid. "All of us except for LuAnn, of course. You know her, don't you? LuAnn Michaels?"

10
ONE WEEK LATER
ASTRID

I stare blankly at the empty classroom. It's 6 a.m. and the girls won't be in for another hour, but I came in because I couldn't sleep. I haven't been able to sleep for a week. It all seems like a dream.

I want to say it seems like a nightmare, but that wouldn't be right. Armand and I are together, and this past week has only made me more sure of it, of him, of us.

Unfortunately, that's the only thing I'm sure about right now. And if we were a normal couple living a normal life, that would be enough. But we aren't a normal couple, and this most certainly isn't shaping up to be a normal life.

"Not unless normal means planning to kill your school-principal boss because she's running a side-gig in human trafficking," I mutter out loud as I stare at the tiny vial sitting on my desk, right next to an apple that little Paulina brought for me two days ago.

The vial contains a neurotoxin—a synthetic poison that Gus told us was making its way around criminal circles because it's virtually undetectable in an autopsy. It paralyzes the heart muscles, causing immediate cardiac arrest. Yup. Makes it look like the victim just up and died. Doesn't even need to be injected into a vein, Gus told me. Just a few drops in a cup of tea will do it. Pretty much destroys the hit-man business, he'd quipped to Armand, who wasn't amused in the least.

Indeed, Armand's been going crazy after I agreed to do this and Gus let us go back to our daily routines.

"You aren't going to take a life," he told me the other day, shaking his head like it was his choice, not mine. "You don't know what it'll do to you, Astrid."

"How can I walk away knowing what I know about LuAnn?!" I shot back, not sure if I was indignant that he was underestimating me or just scared . . . scared of myself!

"You don't know Gus like I do," he'd said. "He's a master manipulator. Can bluff his way in and out of Fort Knox if he wanted, with gold ingots sticking out of his pockets. He made his first million playing poker in the underground dens! He's playing you. Playing both of us! Fuck knows why he wants LuAnn dead, but that's his problem, not ours."

"If LuAnn's really doing what Gus says she's doing, then it's *my* problem!" I screamed at him, ignoring the madness of the fact that my hitman fiancé was trying to talk me out of murdering someone! How the hell had my life taken such a turn in just a week!

Fate, I think as I stare at that apple and cock my head. I blink as I look at the vial again, glancing back at the apple. Then I take a breath and reach into my bag for the small syringe. I tear open the package, pull out the syringe, and with trembling fingers slide it into the mouth of the vial. I draw out a lethal dose of the poison, and with a slow breath plunge the needle through the skin of the apple. I inject the poison into the red fruit, my heart racing as this shit suddenly gets real.

"You going to eat that?" comes a voice from behind me, and I drop the syringe on the table and turn so fast I almost stumble. It's LuAnn, and from the way she's looking at me with her cold blue eyes, I know the game is up and I've lost. Of course I've lost! What the hell was I thinking! I don't know how LouAnn knows, but she knows. Maybe she had a spy in Gustav's house. A snitch in Gustav's crew. Whatever it is, she knows, and I'm done for. Seriously, what did I expect?! I'm a goddamn fourth-grade teacher! Just because I spread my fat thighs for a killer doesn't mean I can suddenly flip a switch and become a goddamn Mata Hari assassin!

"Red and delicious," says LuAnn as she strolls around to the front of the table, where the vial and syringe are staring up at her like the little tattletales they are. "Lots of sugar, though. It'll go straight to your hips." She takes a breath and looks into my eyes, and I know immediately that everything Gus told me about her is true. "Or straight to your heart," she whispers, picking up the apple and holding it up. "Go on, Mrs. Astrid. Take a bite."

I take a step away from her, the back of my thighs bumping against my wooden chair. I stare at the apple and then back into LuAnn's blue eyes. Common sense tells me I need to fight, punch her in the goddamn face, run for my life! But for some reason I don't feel like I'm about to die. I just want to understand. I need to understand.

"How could you?" I say to her, shaking my head slowly. "How could you even . . ."

"Oh, grow up," LuAnn says, snorting at me and tossing her hair back. "It's not as bad as it sounds."

"Selling girls to the highest bidder? *Our* girls?!"

LuAnn shakes her head and sighs like I'm some idealistic moron. "Every girl is for sale, Astrid. That's how it's always been. If our parents don't sell us off, then we sell ourselves to the guy who gives us what we want." She pauses as I stare at her like she's insane—which, by the way, she is. "And for the record, I don't sell to the highest bidder. I vet all my buyers carefully. I send my girls to good homes. To good men."

My mouth hangs open. "A good man doesn't buy little girls from insane cunts like you."

"Whoa! Language!" says LuAnn, raising her arms in mock horror. "Your precious little girls will be rolling in at any minute." She pauses and looks back at the apple in her hand. "Every little girl except for Paulina. She gave you this apple, didn't she? A goodbye gift, right?"

A chill rushes through me as I stare at the apple. LuAnn is right. Paulina gave me the apple two days ago. She told me her family was moving out of state and this Friday would be her last day.

"You're lying," I whisper as that chill rises to the point where I can barely stand. I feel my fists clenching, my blood heating up. Now I think that hell yeah, I *could* kill! What's more, I don't need some space-age poison. I'll just straight-up *strangle* the bitch!

"Am I? Here," LuAnn says, pulling out her phone and tapping on it. "Talk to Paulina's parents. Ask to speak to Paulina. See what they say."

I blink as I stare at the phone, my mind swirling with everything LuAnn just told me. Vetted buyers. And vetted sellers too?! Of course! That's how Lu-Ann managed to do this under the radar! She wasn't having little girls kidnapped and shipped off to sex dungeons or whorehouses! She was working with consenting parents, matching sellers with buyers like an evil broker in a human marketplace! If parents sold their children willingly, then took the money and moved away from friends and family, no one would ever know the kid was gone, would they? Sure, the government could audit them or the freakin' census bureau could look into it, but why would they unless there was a red flag or someone complained?!

"I only accept parents who don't have extended families," LuAnn says as if she's describing a goddamn insurance policy. "Nobody who's going to raise the alarm that this family had a kid a week ago and now the kid is gone. They move a few states away, start a new life." She shrugs and chuckles. "Maybe even have a new kid. I've had a couple of repeat customers over the years, actually."

"You're insane," I stammer, looking at the phone and knowing I don't need to call Paulina's parents to know that they'll make up some excuse why Paulina can't come to the phone.

"I'm providing a service," says LuAnn, shaking her

head. "My customers are rich, powerful men from all over the world. You think they can't find other ways to get what they want? At least this way I'm making it easier for the girls. Would you rather they get kidnapped, brutalized, broken in before getting shipped to their new masters in a cage?"

"*You* need to be in a cage!" I scream, but the moment I take a step towards her, LuAnn reaches beneath her jacket and pulls out a small gun, stopping me dead in my tracks.

I'm about to say to hell with it and go for her anyway, go out fighting, maybe even get a good punch in before I'm shot down. No way LuAnn is letting me walk away after everything she's told me. This is the end of the game. The end of my story.

My eyes tear up as I think about the past week with Armand. Even with the madness of what was happening, we'd found time to be with each other. We'd taken walks by the lake. We'd eaten at sidewalk cafes. Visited the aquarium. Strolled arm in arm through a sea of roses at the botanical gardens. And we'd made love. God, we'd made love!

It's like my whole life is flashing before my eyes as I prepare to launch myself at LuAnn, and even when I see Armand's massive body come crashing through the classroom window like a wrecking ball, it feels like everything's happening in slow motion.

LuAnn whips around, squeezing the trigger furiously as Armand roars and leaps at her. I scream as I see the bullets rip through the skin on his massive arms, but he's on her before she scores a mortal shot. With one swipe of his hand he knocks her gun across the room, and when I get to him he's got her pinned between his strong thighs, his gun pressed against her forehead.

"Look away, Astrid," he says without turning to me. I can see that his expression is cold, that he's flipped that switch that allowed him to do what he did for so long and still keep that other side of him alive, that side that came out for me, the part of him that's tender, the part of him that's loving, the part of him that's mine.

"No," I say, completing my train of thought out loud. "This part of you is mine too, Armand. I love all of you. And I want to understand all of you." I swallow hard as I try to fight back the words I feel coming. This man is about to cross a line he's never crossed. Cross it for me. Shouldn't I be willing to do the same for him?

"No," I say again, this time with more confidence. I go to Armand and put my hand on his shoulder. "Give me the gun."

"She needs to die, Astrid," Armand says through gritted teeth. "And I don't even give a shit what she's done to those girls. She needs to die just for threatening you."

"Yeah, well, I'm not having you spend your life in prison for this bitch," I say to him even as a strange thrill rises up in me from what Armand just said. And he was totally serious, wasn't he? Just pointing a gun at his woman pretty much drew a death sentence from my hitman! Now *that's* romance!

Armand blinks, the rage slowly leaving him as if he'd only just realized that it'd be pretty tough to explain blowing the school principal's brains out in a fourth-grade classroom, no matter what the circumstances might be.

"Besides," I say, caressing his shoulders as I see I'm getting through to him, stopping my killer of a fiancé from losing himself to his killer instinct. "She's got a list of men who are in the market for buying young girls. Maybe records of all the girls she's sold. Those names need to get to the FBI. To Interpol. To the goddamn *New York Times*!"

Armand breaks a grin and nods. Then he sighs and pulls the gun away from LuAnn's head before sitting back on her legs so she still can't move. He looks at me, and I stare dreamily into his eyes like this is a totally romantic moment, something we'll tell our grandkids during Thanksgiving.

I want to kiss my man, but I'm distracted by movement. Quickly I turn to LuAnn, afraid she's reached for her gun.

Then I gasp when I see she's reached for the other weapon in the room.

The apple.

The apple that I laced with poison.

Armand is still looking at me, and then I realize he must not have seen what I did to the apple! He must have been following LuAnn all this while, splitting time between watching me and her!

"Armand, stop her!" I shriek.

Armand frowns, his head turning towards LuAnn's gun, which is still safely across the room. Then he stares back at LuAnn, who's holding the apple up to her mouth.

"What the fuck?" he says, totally confused. "Are you—"

"I'm not spending my life in a jail cell, getting raped by some prison guard or a gang of butch lesbians," she whispers to me as she takes a crisp bite and swallows just as Armand knocks the apple away.

"Why not? You were doing the same for those girls, weren't you?" I snap back, feeling a sick sense of satisfaction go through me when I realize that this is justice, this is what needs to happen—not just for her, but for me. I need to understand what it feels like to take a life. It's the only way I'll be fully bonded to the man that fate has linked me with. The only way I'll fully accept even the darkness in him:

By realizing that I'm capable of that same darkness.

By showing him that I'm his equal, that I'm his woman, that I'm his.

I'm his, I think as I look into Armand's eyes while LuAnn dies quietly in the background, like she's meaningless.

I'm his, I think again as I realize that this wasn't about LuAnn, it wasn't about justice, it wasn't about anything but me and him, two people coming together, two people dealing with whatever was thrown at them, two people fighting for their happily ever after.

This was my story, I think as Armand stands and rushes over to me.

This was our story, I decide as I feel his warm kisses smother me.

This is our happy ending, I realize as I glance down at his wounds even as he carries me out of the room.

Our happy ending.

Always and forever.

∞

EPILOGUE 1
ONE MONTH LATER
ASTRID

Mrs. Astrid's getting married! Mrs. Astrid's getting married! Mrs. Astrid's getting married!

I glance over at the small gathering of teachers, parents, and pretty much *all*my girls, even those I taught years ago. I'm blushing bright red in my white wedding gown, and my heart is so full I wonder if I'm going to pass out before I walk down the aisle.

Gustav is walking me down the aisle, and I look over at the old mafia mob boss who's dressed in a shining suit that looks expensive. He's holding a box, and I know it's my ring. After all, Gustav is also playing the role of Armand's best man!

I look down the aisle and see Armand. He looks tall and broad in his groom's suit, his hair freshly cropped, stubble carefully manicured. I still can't believe everything that's happened over the past month, but I tell myself it doesn't matter whether I believe it or not.

Because it's happened.

Holy shit, this is happening!

The opening chords of *Here Comes the Bride* rings out through the hall, and I look back to my one flower-girl. It's Paulina, bright-eyed and cherub faced, saved from her "buyer" by the FBI before the sick asshole had a chance to destroy her innocence. In that moment I know I've made a difference in a way I wouldn't have if not for Armand, if not for that choice I'd made to cross the street and walk through his door, if not for the choice he'd made to take me as his woman at first sight, to claim me with the confidence of a man who knows what he wants, to claim me curves and all, curvy and all.

Armand looks back at me, his gaze moving up along my curves as I swing my hips like it's nobody's business. This is my wedding, I think as I look into Armand's eyes and put one foot in front of the other, walking confidently towards my waiting husband, the man who'll always wait for me, always protect me, always love me just as I am, perfect as I am, curvy as I am.

Just as I'll always be there for him.

Curvy for him.

EPILOGUE 2
__EIGHT MONTHS LATER__
__ARMAND__

I glance at my curvy wife's pregnant belly, and then up at the calendar on the wall. It's got tomorrow's date circled on it. Tomorrow we see our twins in the flesh.

Yeah, it's twins. A boy and a girl. We don't have names for them yet. We decided we're going to see them before naming them.

"They published the names this morning," Astrid says, looking up from the small laptop she's got perched on her beautiful belly. "Almost a hundred names, Armand! Billionaires and politicians from around the world! Even the ones that the FBI can't charge with a crime will have their lives destroyed!"

I nod. Three months ago the FBI's technicians cracked the encryption on LuAnn's computers and found her secret lists. They were able to track down all the girls LuAnn had sold over the years, ranging from kids all the way to some who were grown women with children of their own! I can't even think about that shit without feeling sick to my stomach, especially as I'm about to become a dad myself!

"I don't want you reading that stuff right now," I say, taking the laptop away from her. "That part of our lives is over and done with. I don't want you getting stressed out in this state. It could impact our unborn children, you know."

Astrid snorts, shaking her head and smiling. Her pretty round cheeks are glowing from her imminent entry into motherhood, and she looks divine. I let my gaze drift down to her boobs, which are swollen with her milk. I've seen her oozing through the thick cotton of her maternity bras, and it's embarrassed me to find that I get hard like a perverted beast as I fantasize about suckling on her while I fuck her with everything I've got. Of course, I don't dare put my cock inside her when she's in this fragile state. She's been satisfying me with her warm mouth and her soft hands the best she can, but there's nothing like the feeling of her warm pussy around my cock.

"Um, I think you're the only that's stressed," she says, teasing me with her eyes. "Come here. Bring it here. I'll help you relax."

She wriggles upright, leaning against the backboard of our king-sized bed. She licks her lips, and I groan as she unclasps her bra from the front, letting her swollen boobs hang out in a way that almost makes me come in my pants.

"Twist my arm," I grunt as I unbuckle and unzip, tossing away my pants and straddling her. My cock throbs against her breasts, and I groan as she squeezes my shaft with her heavy boobs. "Oh, fuck, babe. Your boobs . . . oh, hell, babe."

"You want a taste?" she whispers, looking up at me.

"What? No! That's sick," I say, even though the way my cock hardens between her tits tells her I'm lying.

She giggles. "I've seen how hard you get when I'm milking myself to release the pressure," she says, looking at me knowingly. She frowns and looks down at herself, pinching her big red nipples until her cream starts to flow. "Come to think of it, I'm feeling some pressure right now."

I can't hold myself back any longer, not with Astrid looking so goddamn hot from this angle, her big boobs hanging off to the sides, her round belly swollen with my babies, her thick thighs splayed out on our bed. So with a groan I descend on her, taking her left nipple into my mouth and sucking so hard I get a hot jet of her sweet milk right down my gullet!

She shrieks as I drink from her, suckling from one boob and then the other until she's moaning and writhing. I finger her cunt as I bite and suck her boobs, feeling her divine wetness flow down my hand, past my goddamn wrist! I want to fuck her so bad it hurts, but it's too far along in the pregnancy. I'll just have to wait. I'll just have to make do with another handjob or my wife's perfect lips. Wow, life is hard, ain't it?!

But then Astrid slides down flat on the bed and turns, rising up on her knees and sticking her ass up in the air. I stare in shock as she spreads her big bottom for me, exposes her shining rear pucker, clean and dark. I'm fucking drooling her milk, my cock throbbing as I wonder if this is really happening. Over the past nine months I've teased her there, fingered her rim until she moaned, even made her come once just from that. But we never went further. I could tell she was hesitant, wasn't sure if she could take me.

"Babe, do you know what you're doing?" I mutter

his thick semen following his exit, dripping down my crack and onto the bed, which thankfully has been fitted with a waterproof liner. Giving each other what we need, when we need it? It might horrify society, but we live in a society that would frown at something as natural as a woman breastfeeding in public!

So to hell with society, I think as my big hitman-killer of a husband collapses next to me and places his hands on my belly as our twins playfully kick for Daddy. This is how we start a new society, isn't it? By having babies. Raising them with love. Love for themselves, for their bodies!

Yes, I think as I look at that circled date and feel the excitement of seeing our twins come out of me tomorrow. It starts with us.

With our story.

With our always.

With our forever.

∞

Made in the USA
San Bernardino, CA
05 January 2020

62699219R00058